# Usborne
# Illustrated
# Stories
## for
# Girls

# Usborne
# Illustrated
# Stories
## for
# Girls

Designed by Helen Wood
Cover design by Zöe Wray
Edited by Lesley Sims
and Louie Stowell

# CONTENTS

# The Princess
## and the Pea

Once upon a time there was a prince
who wanted to marry a princess.
But he didn't want just any old
princess. He wanted a real one.

Not one of the local princesses would do.
"What's the matter with them, Patrick?"
cried his father, the king. "I'm running out
of princesses to show you."

Are they too old? Too tall?

Too hairy?

"I can't be sure they're real," sighed Prince Patrick. "I'll have to find one for myself."

"You must do whatever you want, darling," said the queen, who spoiled him rotten. "Nothing but the best for my princey-wincey."

MOTHER!

The next day Prince Patrick set out to travel the world, in search of a real princess.

Errrr... I think my arm's stuck.

He took with him twelve suitcases, ten pairs of shoes, a spare crown and his cousin, Fred.

"Goodbye, my love," cried the queen,
wiping away a tear with her silk handkerchief.
"Don't forget to wrap up warm!"

And brush your teeth!

Stop
FUSSING,
Mother!

They hadn't gone far when they heard
a loud sneeze from under the seat.
"Who's there?" shouted the prince.
A small figure crept out.

It's Peg!

"Aren't you the palace maid?"
said Prince Patrick.

Peg nodded.

"Well, what are you doing here?"
the prince asked.

"I want to see the world," said Peg.
"I've been at the palace all my life – ever
since I was left on the doorstep as a baby."

She blushed. "And Cook's furious
because I burned the pudding," she added.

"Well you can't come with us," said Fred. "This is a boys-only adventure. You'll get scared and want to go home."

No I won't! I'm as brave as you.

"We're not turning back now," said Prince Patrick. "She'll have to join us."

Peg grinned at Fred.

"OK," Prince Patrick went on. "First stop, the wicked witch's hut."

"You're joking?" cried Fred in alarm.

She'll eat us ALIVE!

Prince Patrick shook his head. "The witch will know how to find a real princess. She's my best hope..."

"Now Peg," said Prince Patrick, "this could be dangerous. You stay in the coach. Fred and I will meet the witch."

The prince knocked three
times on the witch's door...
There was no answer.

"Looks like no one's in. We'll have to go,"
said Fred, who was already backing away.

"She must be in," said the prince, and he
bent down to peer through the keyhole.

A large green eye was staring at him.
Prince Patrick jumped back and landed
bottom-first in a patch of mud.

18

A short plump woman opened the door, chuckling to herself. "Did I scare you? I was just checking who you were. You can't be too careful these days."

Fred was amazed. "Are you the witch?" he asked. "You're not scary at all."

The witch looked rather upset. "I try my best," she sighed. "I grew three new warts last week."

"Come inside," she added. "I'm just cooking some tasty soup for lunch."

Subthig REALLY sbells in here.

"We're not hungry," said Prince Patrick quickly. "I've come to ask for your help. I want to know how to find a real princess."

"Real princesses are very rare," said the witch, "and it's hard to spot a fake one. But there is a test you can do."

*Hmmm... Let me see...*

"A real princess must have... boiled brains, rotten beans and cat spit."

"What?" cried the prince.

"Oh sorry, that's a recipe for soup. This is it..."

The real princess test

A real princess must possess ...

1. Politeness to one and all

2. Kindness to rich and poor

3. Very sensitive skin

"Sensitive skin?" Prince Patrick asked, looking confused.

"A real princess," explained the witch, "has such tender skin that she could feel a pea under twenty mattresses."

"Thank you," said the prince. "You've been very helpful." He turned to the door.

"Oh do stay for lunch," pleaded the witch. "My soup's almost ready. And bring in that poor girl from outside."

No... really, thanks!

Urrgh!! I can't eat THAT!

They were stuck in the witch's hut until the cauldron was empty.

"I feel sick," groaned Peg on the way back to the coach.

"Well, you shouldn't have had three bowls then," said Fred.

"I was being polite! I didn't want to hurt the witch's feelings."

"That was very kind of you, Peg," said Prince Patrick, smiling at her.

"Where are we going now?" asked Fred.
"Now I have the witch's test, I can finally find
a real princess," said the prince. "We're off to
meet Princess Prunella. Check the map, Fred."

Princess Prunella was very excited to see the prince. "You must come and stay in my castle," she cried. She raced over the bridge, dragging Prince Patrick with her.

"Hurry! Hurry!" she called to
her servants. "I want you to
prepare the best bedchambers
for the prince and Fred."

"Excuse me," said Peg, struggling with all the luggage. "Where am I to sleep?"

"Maids belong in the attic," replied the princess, haughtily. "There might be a few mice there, but I'm sure you'll cope."

Peg went to her room. It was cold and damp.
She could hear mice scuttling about, squeaking.

*The prince can't marry her...*

Meanwhile, Fred and the prince were in the
grand dining room with Princess Prunella.

"You're being very kind," said Prince Patrick, "but what about Peg? Is she eating in the kitchen?"

The princess looked shocked. "Your beastly little maid? You can't expect *me* to bother with *her*."

She can eat the
PIG SLOPS
if she's hungry.

"I'm afraid we must leave," said Prince Patrick. "You're not a real princess after all."

"Oh yes I am!" cried Princess Prunella.
"Oh no you're not!" shouted Fred.
"You've failed the first real princess test."

RATS!

"Real princesses are polite to everyone,"
explained Prince Patrick, "and you've just
been rude to Peg."

"I won't give up!" said Prince Patrick. "There must be a real princess somewhere..."

"According to this map, there's a Princess Pavlova next door. Let's try her," Fred suggested.

Princess Pavlova greeted them all very politely. "What a pleasure to have you here," she said. "Welcome to my castle."

"She's passed the politeness test," thought the prince. "Now what's the next one..."

2. Kindness to rich and poor

"Fred!" he cried, "I have a plan. I'm going to dress up as a beggar and see if Princess Pavlova is kind to me."

"Try out your disguise on Peg first," said Fred, "to make sure it works."

Prince Patrick found Peg sitting on a tree stump, about to eat an apple. "I'm a hungry beggar," he said.

Have you any food for me?

"Oh you poor thing!" Peg cried, when she saw him. "Here, have my apple."

Prince Patrick was very pleased with himself. "Excellent! It works," he shouted, throwing off his disguise.

It's YOU!

"What are you doing?" asked Peg. But the prince was already knocking on the castle door, to try the test on Princess Pavlova.

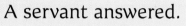

A servant answered.

"Is someone there?" called Princess Pavlova.

"It's a beggar, Your Highness."

"We've got nothing for him," snapped the princess. "Tell him to go away."

And he smells... POO-EE!

Prince Patrick turned away. "She's not a real princess," he thought. "A real princess is both polite and kind – even to beggars."

37

...oh dear!

"I give up," said the prince, with a sigh. "I'll never be married! I don't think there's a real princess anywhere. We may as well go home."

They got ready for the long journey back to the palace. Everyone was glum, even the horses.

"I bet Cook hasn't forgotten about the pudding I burned," thought Peg.

The coach arrived at the palace just in time. A huge storm was brewing.

Peg was sent straight to the kitchens in disgrace. "You've got hundreds of dishes to wash," scolded the cook. "They've been piling up since you left."

Prince Patrick and Fred went to find the king and queen. Outside, rain began beating against the windows. Streaks of lightning lit up the sky.

Just then, there was a knock on the door.
"There is a Princess Primrose to see you,
Your Highness," said the footman.

A beautiful princess stepped into the
room. She was wet from the rain and
shaking with cold.

"I'm so sorry to trouble you,"
she said politely, "but my coach
has broken down."

"No trouble at all," said Prince Patrick quickly. "Why don't you stay the night at our castle? We'll fix your coach in the morning."

I must give you something in return!

"She acts like a real princess," thought the prince, "but I must be sure."

3. Very sensitive skin

He asked the servants
to prepare Princess Primrose's
bedroom.

"I want twenty mattresses on
the bed," ordered Prince Patrick,
"and a pea at the very bottom."

Peg didn't get to bed that night.
She had to finish washing the dishes.

The next morning, Princess Primrose came down for breakfast, looking refreshed.

"How did you sleep?" asked Prince Patrick.

I slept like a baby.

"I loved all those mattresses," the princess said. "It was the most comfortable bed."

Prince Patrick sighed. "A real princess would have felt that pea," he thought. He waved goodbye to Princess Primrose as soon as breakfast was over. "Another fake one," he said, sadly.

It was Peg's job to clean the princess's bedroom. Slowly, she climbed up the ladder, yawning with each step. "I'll just lie down for a moment," Peg thought, "before I start cleaning up."

Zzzzzzzzz

In no time at all, she was fast asleep.

An hour later, Peg woke with a start. "Ow!" she said. "There's something really lumpy in this bed. I'm getting down."

Oooh! It's a long way down!

But as she leaned over, she knocked the ladder. It clattered to the ground. "Drat!" Peg cried. "I'm stuck."

"Help!" she shouted, as loudly as she could,
"I'm stuck. Please... HELP!"
Everyone rushed into the bedroom.

"What are you doing up there?" Prince
Patrick called.
"I was supposed to be cleaning," said Peg,
"but I was so tired I fell asleep."

"And there's something horribly hard in this bed," she added. "I'm covered in bruises."

Prince Patrick knew this could only mean one thing...

Yeek!

"I can't believe it!" cried the prince. "You were polite to the witch, kind to a beggar and now you've felt a pea under twenty mattresses. You must be a real princess!"

He raced up the ladder.
"Peg, will you marry me?"
Peg gasped. "You want to marry me,
a palace maid? Yes please!"

A MAID!?

But a princess
at heart my
dear!

So Prince Patrick finally married his real princess. He put the pea in a glass case in the palace museum for everyone to see.

Ye Royal pea

It may still be there today...

# The doll's house

Amy and Tina loved Cherry Tree Cottage.
"It's the prettiest doll's house ever," said Tina.

"And Molly's the best doll's owner,"
Amy added. "We're so lucky to live here."

"You may feel lucky," said Cordelia. "I don't!"
Cordelia was a beautiful doll and she knew it.

She had golden curls tied up with a shiny clip and a dress that sparkled with sequins.

"I don't belong here," said Cordelia, "I should be in a doll's palace. Not stuck in this stuffy, boring cottage."

"It's boring because you never do anything," said Amy. "You never help clean or tidy."

"I have more important things to do," snapped Cordelia. "Like brushing my hair."

 55

"Please stop fighting," said Tina. And they had to, as just then they heard Molly.

RUN!

The dolls rushed back to where Molly had left them and stayed as still as they could.

"It's a sunny day," Molly told them, "so I'm taking you all on a picnic."

She carefully picked up the dolls and put them in her basket.

"Oh dear," sighed Cordelia, as Molly set them down on an old rug. "I hope my dress doesn't get dirty."

"Look at your sequins and your clip," Tina whispered, to cheer her up. "They're sparkling in the sun."

But far above in the sky, a magpie had spotted Cordelia too. Like all magpies, he loved collecting sparkly things.

The next moment, he
swooped down and snatched
Cordelia up in his claws.

HEY!
Let me GO!

Cordelia screamed, but the magpie didn't
stop. He flew on and on, higher and higher.

♥ 59 ♥

At last they came to a tall tree. The magpie dropped Cordelia into his spiky nest.

"Take me back this second," ordered Cordelia.

The magpie shook his head.
"You're mine now," he said, then flew away on his bright, glossy wings.

"Oh!" cried Cordelia. "This is horrible."
She spent all day in the nest, feeling
lonelier and lonelier. "Please help me,"
she called to a passing magpie.

Oh no,
I'm ruined!

"Only if you give me your shiny clip,"
said the magpie.

"I'll give you anything you want," sobbed Cordelia. "Just take me home."

At Cherry Tree Cottage, Molly was putting Amy and Tina to bed. "I'll never see Cordelia again," she thought, sadly.

Suddenly, there was a shout.

"Molly!" called her mother. "Look who I found by the back door!"

There, in the palm of her hand, sat Cordelia. Her curls were ragged and wild and her dress was dirty and torn.

"Cordelia!" cried Molly, carefully tucking her into bed. "I can't believe you're back."

"Nor can I," said Amy, once Molly had left. "I thought you hated Cherry Tree Cottage."

"It's no palace," Cordelia said, "but it's much better than a bird's nest. Anyway," she added sadly, "I've lost my sparkle now."

"Never mind," said Amy. "At least you won't be stolen by a magpie again."

# The tooth fairy

It was a fantastic day for Crystal.
She had passed her final test at
the tooth fairy training school.

Now she could turn children's baby
teeth into money.

Jet, Crystal's lazy classmate, had failed
all her tests. She would never be
a tooth fairy. "It's not fair!"
she moaned.

As Jet grumbled, the others
flew home and prepared for
their first trips.

That night, Crystal checked that she had everything she needed...

one bag of magic travel dust...

*Check!*

*Check!*

one list of children to visit...

and, most importantly, her wand.

*Check!*

Crystal sprinkled herself with magic dust. The next second, she was in the bedroom of her first customer, Beth Bingly.

Crystal flew up to the bed. Carefully, she lifted a tooth out from under Beth's pillow.

She aimed her wand at Beth's tooth.
"*Zapanasha!*" she cried. But instead of
a shiny, new coin, she saw...

A ham sandwich?

A hamster?

A CACTUS?

Every time she aimed her wand, the tooth
changed into something – but never a coin.

Crystal burst into tears. "It's all gone wrong," she sobbed.

Her crying woke Beth, who couldn't believe her eyes.

"Are you the tooth fairy?" she whispered in amazement.

"Yes," wept Crystal, "but it's my first night and I'm useless."

Crystal explained how her wand had failed.
"Everyone in Fairyland will laugh at me,"
she sobbed. "What can I do?"

Beth felt sorry for the fairy.
"Let me go back with you,"
she said. "Maybe I can help."

"Thank you," Crystal sniffed.

A sprinkle of travel dust later, Beth was in Fairyland. The magic powder had made her fairy-sized. She could fly, too!

"My wand came from the Fantastic Fairy Store," explained Crystal.

"Then we'll start there," said Beth.

Beth gasped as she entered the shop. The walls were lined with hundreds of fairy outfits.

There were sparkly tiaras, silky bows, shiny shoes and pots and pots of gleaming wands.

"How can I help you?" asked the shopkeeper.

Crystal explained and the shopkeeper examined the wand.

"This is Jet's wand," she said. "It will never work properly, because she's such a bad fairy."

"That sneaky fairy has swapped her wand for mine," cried Crystal.

"Let's get it back," said Beth.

Jet was lazing on the terrace of her tree house. She'd used Crystal's wand to magic up a huge pile of cream cakes.

She was just about to gulp down her tenth eclair, when Crystal and Beth arrived.

"Hand over my wand, you thief!" demanded Crystal.

"No way, Miss Perfect," said Jet. A stream
of stars shot from the wand in her hand.
The magical blast turned Crystal's
feet to stone.

Jet raised the wand to strike again.
But suddenly it was snatched from her grasp.
"I'll take that," cried Beth, from a branch
above Jet's head.

Jet tried to fly up and grab the wand back. But she'd eaten so much, she couldn't get off the ground.

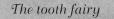

A second blast from the wand lifted the stony spell from Crystal's feet. She fluttered up to join Beth. "So long, Jet!" cried Crystal as they flew away.

The pair returned to the Fantastic Fairy Store. Crystal bought Beth her very own fairy outfit to thank her.

Then Beth joined the fairies for a midnight feast and they danced until dawn.

"Time to say goodbye," said Crystal, showering Beth in magic dust.

In a flash, Beth was back in bed. "What an amazing dream," she thought.

Beth peeked under her pillow. She expected to see her tooth, or even a coin. But what she saw was the tiniest dress in the world.

# The Little Mermaid

Far out at sea,
below the waves,
deeper
and deeper
and deeper still,
stood the
Sea King's castle.

There, at the very bottom of the sea, the water was as clear as glass. The sand was as fine as powder. Tall seaweed grew up around the castle walls and small, bright fish darted among its branches.

The Sea King was very proud of his
castle. It was the perfect place to
bring up his six mermaid daughters.

Each daughter was given her
own small garden to care for.
"I'm going to shape mine like
a whale," said the eldest.

"Mine will have a
seashell border,"
said the next.

"And I'm going to grow
pretty flowers," said the third.

★ 84 ★

The fourth and fifth mermaids loved exploring. "Let's decorate our gardens with treasure from shipwrecks," they said.

Then their little sister appeared, hugging a statue of a smiling boy. "Look what I've found!" she cried. "I'm going to put him in my garden."

The sisters spent all day in the castle waters, tending their gardens and playing games. In the evening, as the sea turned to inky black, their grandmother called them inside for supper.

Mermaids!

Lying on silky cushions, the family ate steaming seaweed parcels and soft sea fruits.

"Tell us a story, Grandmama,"
begged the littlest mermaid.

Grandmama had seen the world
above the waves. She told amazing
tales of men with two legs and no tail.

"There are buildings as tall as the ocean
is deep," she said, "and machines that
glide even faster than sharks."

The little mermaid hung on her every word. "When you reach fifteen," announced the Sea King, "you may rise above the waves and see these things for yourselves."

While the older sisters flicked their tails in delight, the little mermaid sat drumming her fingers. "That's six whole years away!" she sighed.

On the eldest sister's fifteenth birthday, the Sea King's castle frothed with excitement.

The mermaids showered their big sister with twinkling pearls. But the best present of all was the Sea King's blessing.

"Now you can swim to the surface of the sea," he said.

"Come back quickly!" called the little
mermaid. She wanted to hear everything
about the world above.

Her sister finally returned, grinning
with excitement. "I watched the sun
sink into the sea," she said. "Its
orange light flooded the water."

Oooooooooh!

Oooooooooooooh!

Oooooooooh!

Were you afraid?

Did you see land?

Were there any boats?

For hours, the mermaids pestered
her with questions. Her littlest sister
was the most curious. "Did the wind
stroke your hair?" she asked. "Did the
sun kiss your cheeks?"

That night, the little mermaid gazed at the sea above. A black blot glided through the water.

"It must be a ship!" she thought. "I wonder who's on it and where they're going…?" She fell asleep and dreamed of sailing the ocean.

*I wonder what air feels like?*

One by one, the sisters reached fifteen and were allowed to swim above the waves. The little mermaid watched them rise up, hand in hand, longing for the day she could join them.

As time dragged on, the little mermaid spent hours with her statue. "I can't wait to see what dry land looks like," she told him.

Finally, the year... then the month... then the day of her fifteenth birthday arrived. As soon as the celebrations were over, she set off for the surface.

"Goodbye!" she called to her sisters, rising up like a bubble of air. With each swish of her tail, the water felt lighter.

Her head broke through the waves and she gasped. The sun was setting, just as her sister had described. And there, ahead, floated a ship.

The little mermaid swam closer. Lanterns hung
from the masts and lively music filled the air.
Closer still, she saw people dancing on deck.

She stared in delight as their two legs
carried them back and forth. A handsome
young man appeared, wearing a crown.

"Happy birthday, Prince Milo!"
the people shouted, as a hundred
rockets exploded in the sky.

The little mermaid watched the prince, enchanted. It was as if her statue had come to life.

Suddenly, the weather turned stormy and everyone ran below deck. Waves rose up like mountains around the creaking ship and a streak of lightning split the dark clouds.

The little mermaid rode the surf
with glee, but then she heard cries
from the ship. The wind and waves
were battering it apart, tossing
terrified people into the foaming sea.

The mermaid was horrified. "They'll never survive without tails," she thought. "Oh, the poor prince. I must find him..."

She searched everywhere,

diving between beams and planks.

At last she saw him, clinging to a broken mast.

She pulled the prince to a sheltered
cove and let the waves wash him ashore.
"Thank you," he murmured.

The little mermaid watched from a clump
of seaweed. As the dawn light warmed the
sky, a pretty girl came and helped the prince
to his feet. Smiling, he looked out to sea,
then walked away.

The little mermaid
floated joyfully
back to the castle.
"How was it?"
her sisters asked
together.
"Beautiful,"
she sighed.

All day, the sisters played in the castle waters.

"Catch!" cried the eldest, throwing a sponge ball.

But the little mermaid was too busy dreaming of walking with her prince.

That night, and every night for a week, she swam back to the cove and gazed longingly at the empty beach.

At dawn, she returned to her statue under the sea. "Will I ever see my prince again?" she asked. The marble boy just smiled.

"Why do you swim to the same place each night?" asked her sisters, one morning. The little mermaid blushed and told them about her prince.

"I've seen that prince," said the eldest
sister. "He lives in a grand palace by the sea."
"Really?" cried the excited little mermaid.
"Show me!"
That evening, all six mermaids rose up
through the sea and swam to the palace.

It stood proud and shiny at the water's edge. As the mermaids watched, a man strode onto the balcony.

"It's my prince!" cried the little mermaid. "Do you think he's looking for me?"

"Don't be silly," said the eldest sister.

Day after day, the little mermaid returned to the palace. Each time, she swam a little closer.

When the prince went sailing, she swam behind him. She prayed for a storm, so she could save him again. But it never came.

Back beneath the waves,
the sisters were decorating
the castle for a summer ball.
"Come and help us,"
they called to the
little mermaid.

She tried to tie ribbons, but she just couldn't concentrate.

"You're not still thinking about that prince, are you?" said her eldest sister.

The little mermaid nodded.

"Remember, he's a man and you're a mermaid," her sister went on. "He will only make you unhappy."

By nightfall, the sea castle looked splendid.
Blue flames rose up from pearly white
shells, lighting the way from the
gardens to the hall.

Guests streamed in,
wearing shimmery
clothes...

...and a fish band sang
gurgling tunes.

The little mermaid pretended to join in, but she couldn't stop thinking of her prince. "I have to do something," she thought. "Maybe the sea witch can help me..."

While her sisters swayed to the fish band's songs, the little mermaid swam away.

It was a dark and dangerous journey to the sea witch's cave. The little mermaid crossed bubbling hot mud...

dodged swirling whirlpools...

...and darted past slimy seaweed arms.

At last, the craggy cave loomed up ahead.
The ugly sea witch stood at the entrance.

"So you want legs to impress a prince,"
she snapped. (The sea witch knew
everything.) "They will cost you dearly."

"But I have nothing to give you,"
said the little mermaid.

"Yes you do," the witch declared. "Your voice."

The little mermaid gulped. "But how will I talk to my prince?" she asked.

"That's not my problem."

The witch started stirring a potion. "This will split your tail in two," she said, "and give you human legs."

"But there are two things you should know," she added. "One, if you drink this potion, you can never go back to your father's castle. And two, if the prince doesn't return your love... you will dissolve into the ocean waves."

The witch stopped stirring and looked up.
"Do you still want to drink it?" she asked.

The little mermaid didn't pause. "I do,"
she replied. They were the last words
she ever spoke.

With a wave of her wand, the witch
added the mermaid's voice to her potion.

By dawn, the little mermaid was sitting on
a sea rock near the palace. In her trembling
hand she held a bottle of the witch's potion.

Suddenly, a door opened and the prince stepped onto his balcony. He stretched, yawned and gazed out to sea.

The sight of the prince made the mermaid bolder. She swallowed the potion, jumped into the water... spluttered, splashed and nearly drowned. Her tail had split into legs.

The prince saw the splashes. "Who's that?" he called. "Somebody help her."

A servant waded in and pulled the little mermaid to safety. Soon she was standing in front of her prince.

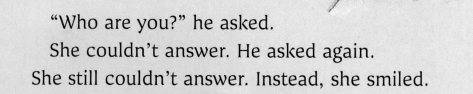

"Who are you?" he asked.

She couldn't answer. He asked again.

She still couldn't answer. Instead, she smiled.

The prince smiled back. "Find this young lady some clothes," he said to his servant. "She's joining me for breakfast."

The little mermaid spent the whole day with the prince. She was very happy but kept wobbling on her new feet.

"Take my arm," said the prince. "I'll show you around."

That evening, the little mermaid stood on the prince's balcony. Frothy waves danced on the rocks below. Five tails flipped by and she recognized her sisters.

"Come back!" they cried.

The little mermaid smiled but shook her head. She had made her choice.

"I don't even know your name," the prince
was saying. "But when I saw you in the water
this morning, I thought of my own true love."

The mermaid's eyes sparkled and her heart
beat faster.

"I almost drowned once," he went on.
"I was swept to a beach and woken by a
lovely princess. Tomorrow I'm going to
set sail and marry her!"

The prince's words were like a dagger in the mermaid's heart. He was everything to her, but he loved someone else.

"Don't worry," he said. "You can come with me."

But the little mermaid shook her head, sobbing silently.

Next morning, she watched her prince sail into the distance.

The world she loved was lost to her.
"You can never go back," said the
witch's voice inside her head.

"Come to us," sang the ocean spray.

"Forever," whispered the foaming surf.
With tears streaming down her cheeks,
the brave little mermaid disappeared into
the welcoming waves.

# The clumsy prince

Colin was the clumsiest prince in the kingdom. Other princes fought dragons. Colin fell over them. Other princes battered villains. Colin bumped into them.

One day, he tripped in front of a sad
princess. She thought he was so funny,
she wanted to marry him on the spot.

Are you princely enough
for my daughter?

Her father had other ideas.
He gave Colin three tests, tests
he knew Colin would not pass.

First, Colin had to show how polite
he could be. But he was so busy talking
politely to the queen...

May I pass
you the sugar,
ma'am?

...that he didn't see the butler.

Next, he had to take the princess out. But somehow, he managed to lose the royal boat.

Eerrr...
Oooops!

Then he had to ride the royal horse like a prince.

"He rides like a clown!" said the king. "He must leave the palace tomorrow."

That night,
Colin couldn't
sleep. Suddenly,
he heard a
scream. It was
the princess!

Help! I'm being kidnapped!

Colin jumped. What was going on? Was someone stealing the princess? He leaned out of his window and sent a flower pot flying...

OOOwwww!

...straight onto the head of the man stealing the princess.

The princess thief fell to the ground with a thud.

Colin raced from the tower and swept up the princess.

Got you!

The king and queen raced out too.
"What's going on?" cried the king.
"What has Clumsy Colin done now?"

"He's rescued me!" said the princess.
"Really?" said the king.
"Really!" she said.

The king smiled. "Well, the reward for rescuing a princess is to marry her," he said.

*Oh, Colin!*

So Colin lived clumsily, but happily ever after.

# The missing pearl

Marina looked at the giant pearl
and sighed. It was the most
beautiful thing she'd ever seen.

According to legend, anyone who owned the pearl would never grow old and could swim the oceans forever. Sharks guarded it day and night.

Giant
Pink Pearl

VIEWINGS DAILY
9am - 5pm

The magical pearl was first prize in King Neptune's Great Seahorse Race.

The event was part of the king's one-hundredth birthday celebrations. Marina was sure that she and her seahorse Swish could win.

Marina had been preparing for months with Scuba, her trainer.

"Make sure Swish has an early night," she told him.

As Marina swam off, a sneaky-looking pair peeked out from behind a rock.

"Our slowcoach of a seahorse won't stand a chance against Swish," whispered Sid the squid. "And Marina is the ocean's best rider."

The mermaid by his side flicked her tail and gave a wicked smile. "We'll see about that," she said.

"What are you going to do, Storm?" asked Sid.

"I have a plan that can't fail," she replied. "That pearl is as good as ours."

Next morning, the seahorses and their riders lined up for the big race. Marina gently stroked Swish's neck. "You can do it, boy," she whispered.

Storm looked across smugly at
Marina. Then she turned and winked
at her trainer.

Sid winked back and swam away.

Hmmm...
What are those two up to?

The prawn starter lowered his flag and they were off.

Soon, Swish and Marina were way ahead of the others.

GO Marina, GO!

But Storm didn't look worried
by Marina's lead.

Ha ha ha ha!

As Marina passed a coral reef, a cloud
of thick, black ink shot out in front of her.
Quick as a flash, Swish leaped over the top.
Marina lost hold of the reins as Swish
sailed over the ink cloud.

The others, spotting the hazard ahead,
swerved quickly past.

"Lucky you're such a good jumper, Swish," said Marina as she took the reins again.

As they raced off, she just spotted an inky tentacle dart back into the coral.

They soon caught up, and were neck and neck with Storm as the finish line came in sight. With a final burst, Swish sped forward to win.

Everyone clustered around to congratulate Marina. Everyone except Storm, that is. She was busy whispering something to Sid, who slithered off quickly.

Three cheers for the winner!

HIP...HIP... HOORAY

HIP...HIP... HOORAY

HIP...HIP... HOORAY!

A few minutes later, they were all in the cabin of the old shipwreck for the prize-giving ceremony.

But they were in for a shock. The pearl
had gone.

The shark guards searched everywhere,
but the pearl was nowhere to be seen.

"It must have been stolen!"
cried Scuba.

"But how?" asked Toothy, the guard.
"This room was locked."

The second guard pointed to a tiny porthole. "That's the only other way in and out."

"But it's too small to get the pearl through," said Sid.

"Then it must have been taken before we locked up," said Toothy.

"Who was the last one alone with the pearl?" asked Storm, with a glint in her eye.

Toothy pointed a fin at Marina.

"She only took part in the race so we wouldn't suspect her," sneered Storm.

"Yeah," added Sid, waving his tentacles. "She only won by chance."

Marina desperately tried to think of a
way to prove her innocence. Suddenly,
Sid's dirty tentacles gave her an idea.

"I think the pearl is still in this room!"
she cried, pointing  at a pile of old cannonballs.
She frantically rubbed each one with her
seaweed necklace.

"Look! This one isn't a cannonball at all," she declared.

"The pearl!" gasped the crowd.

"Covered in squid ink!" added Marina, staring at Sid.

"She made me do it!" cried Sid, pointing at Storm. "I had to disguise the pearl so Storm could collect it later."

"Shush, you stupid squid!" yelled Storm.
But it was too late. The two crooks were
led away and Marina was presented
with her magical pearly prize.

# The twelve dancing princesses

There were once twelve beautiful
princesses, all with long, flowing
hair and short, fiery tempers.

Their father, the king, was
a grumpy old man who
didn't believe in having fun.

All of you just
sit down
and
look pretty!

In fact, he believed that princesses should be seen and not heard.

The princesses strongly disagreed.

The thing they argued about most
was dancing. Their father hated it,
but the princesses loved it...

so whenever
he wasn't looking,
they danced anyway.

The girls slept
in a tall tower with
their beds side by side.

Every night, the king locked the tower door, so that they couldn't sneak out.

*Sleep well...my dears!*

One morning, when the door was unlocked,
the princesses were still asleep.

As the maid went to wake them, she
noticed their shoes were lying in a soggy pile
on the floor.

The shoes were
worn out.

When the king heard about the shoes, he was furious. "Those girls have been out dancing," he spluttered.

"Princesses should not be out dancing all night!" he yelled at them. "You need your beauty sleep. You should all be ashamed of yourselves."

The girls weren't ashamed in the least. What's more, they wouldn't tell him how they had escaped or where they had been.

The next morning, it was clear that the princesses had been out again. The same thing happened seven nights in a row.

The king didn't know what to do.

Then he had a brilliant idea.

He decided that the first man to discover where his daughters went each night could marry one of them. Posters went up across the land.

Fed up with your job? Feel like a challenge?

## Solve a royal mystery and win big prizes!!

### Win your own kingdom and marry a genuine princess!

Interested? Drop in to the castle for further details.

No time-wasters please.

The first man to take up the king's challenge was brave Prince Marcus.

"By the way, there is one small catch," the king told him. "If you fail, I'll cut off your head!"

Um...okay... no problem, your majesty.

That night, Prince Marcus was taken to the tower and put in a room next to the princesses.

They made him very welcome. One even brought him a cup of hot, milky cocoa.

As Prince Marcus drank the
cocoa, he began to feel sleepy.
He tried splashing cold
water on his face, but
that didn't work.

Soon he was fast asleep
and snoring loudly.

Next morning, the princesses' shoes were worn out again. Prince Marcus had failed – and the king wasn't joking about chopping off his head.

Take him
AWAY!

Many more princes and noble knights came forward. But they were all fooled by the princesses' sweet smiles...

Enjoy your drink, sir!

and their offer of hot cocoa.

One day, a magician named Ralph
and his pet dog, Rascal, were
passing the castle.

Ralph noticed one of the king's posters and decided to find out more.

How very interesting, Rascal!

When he saw Ralph, the king looked doubtful. But he was desperate to know what the girls were up to, so he agreed to let Ralph try. "I'll chop off your head if you fail, you know," warned the king.

Yes, but I WON'T fail...

Night came and Ralph was put in the same room where the others had stayed.

"Hello! I'm Amy," said the youngest. "He's nice," she whispered to her sisters. "I don't want him to die because of us. Maybe we shouldn't go out tonight..."

Her sisters ignored her.

A few minutes later, Annabel, the
eldest sister, brought Ralph a cup of
cocoa. But Ralph was a wise magician.
He knew what she was up to.

This is for you...

He pretended to drink the cocoa. Then, when Annabel wasn't looking, he poured it into Rascal's bowl. Rascal was delighted.

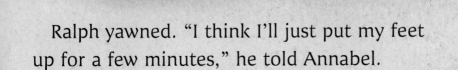

Ralph yawned. "I think I'll just put my feet up for a few minutes," he told Annabel.

Then, with
an even bigger
yawn, he pretended
to fall fast asleep.

Annabel crept back to her
sisters. "He's asleep," she
whispered. "Let's get ready!"
They put on their
sparkliest ball dresses...

and new shoes.
The princesses
shimmered like
a rainbow.

*177*

With the last button buttoned and the
last bow tied, the girls stood by their
beds. Annabel pulled back a dusty,
old rug in the corner of the room
to reveal a secret trap door.
The hinges creaked as she
pulled it open.

One by one the girls disappeared down
some steps and into a long, dark tunnel.

When the princesses were out of sight, Ralph quickly entered their room.

He clicked his fingers
and a cloak appeared.
With a second click,
Ralph vanished.

Carefully, he tiptoed
down the steps into
the tunnel.

It didn't take long for him to catch
up with the princesses.

Ralph tried to walk quietly, but it wasn't easy. At one point he stepped on Amy's dress. She jumped and turned around, but there was no one there...

A few moments later Ralph stepped
on a twig. Now Amy was convinced
that someone was following them.
Her sisters didn't believe her.

CRACK!

What was that?

Nothing, don't be silly!

At the end of the tunnel they came to an astonishing row of trees.

Some of the trees glistened with silver...

some with gold...

and some with sparkling diamonds.

Ralph had never seen trees like them.
While the princesses carried on, he
gently broke off a twig from each tree.

Up ahead, the princesses had
stopped before a lake. It stood in
the shadow of a beautiful castle.

Twelve boats were
waiting at the edge
of the lake and in
each boat sat a
handsome prince.

Each prince rowed a
princess across the lake.

Ralph sneaked into the boat carrying
Amy. When they reached the other
side, a band began to play.

The princesses danced until their
feet were sore and the soles of their
shoes were worn through.

As the sun rose, they limped home. "Our nights of dancing are still safe – unlike poor Ralph's head!" said Annabel, yawning.

Amy looked upset.

The king was having breakfast when
Ralph strolled in. "Good morning,
Your Majesty," said Ralph brightly.

"I suppose you've come to tell me
you failed too," sighed the king.

"Ah, but I didn't, sire," Ralph replied.
Waving the twigs, he told the king
what he'd seen.

"This all sounds very unlikely," grumbled the king, when Ralph had finished. "Are you sure you're not just making it up to save your head?"

He decided to call for Annabel.
When she saw the three twigs in
his hand, she looked horrified.

One look at her face told the king all he
needed to know. "Dancing is banned!"
he declared.

The princesses sobbed and wailed when they heard their secret had been discovered.

"What will we do?" they cried. "Life is so dull without dancing."

But there was nothing they could do.

True to his word, the king let Ralph marry one of his daughters. "I'd like Amy," Ralph said, "if she'll have me. She's the sweetest of all."

Amy and Ralph's wedding was a joyful
occasion. Even the king couldn't stop
smiling. "I have a surprise for you,"
he whispered to Amy.

The king led her to the ballroom and Amy gasped. Hundreds of candles lit up the dance floor and in the corner a band was playing a lively tune.

"As it's a special occasion, you may all dance – but for one night only!" said the king.

"Oh, how wonderful!" cried Amy and
her sisters, grabbing partners. They were
all still dancing the following night.

"I thought I said one night only!"
said the king, but he smiled. Ralph
had worked some more of his magic.

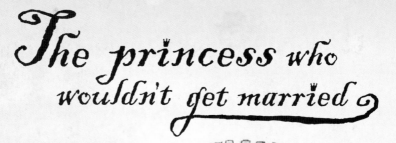

# The princess who wouldn't get married

Prue liked being a princess, except for one thing. She didn't want to marry a prince.

"You have to," said her dad. "It's what princesses do."

The king asked three princes to visit. "Choose one," he told Prue.

But Prue didn't want to. "Princes are boring!" she said.

TOO PLUMP!

TOO TALL!

Prue did like the third prince.
But she didn't say so.

TOO...
HAIRY!

The king was very angry. "If you won't marry a prince..."

...you'll marry
the **first** man
who comes to the castle!

The very next day, a beggar arrived, playing an old violin. "I order you to marry my daughter," barked the king.

Yes sir, your majesty.

Prue and the beggar were married on the spot.

With his beard, the beggar reminded Prue of someone. Whoever he was, she didn't want to marry him. But the beggar took Prue home as his wife.

Welcome to your new home!

"Cheer up!" he said. "If you married a prince, you'd have to live in a boring castle."

The beggar was kind, but very poor. They wore old rags and never had enough to eat. Prue was used to servants. Now, she did everything herself. "The floors at the palace seemed to stay clean on their own," she thought, with a heavy sigh.

One day, the beggar brought home some straw. "We can make baskets to sell," he said. But the straw cut Prue's hands.

"This is no good," thought the beggar.

"You must get a job," he said. "Prince Alec is getting married. Perhaps you can work in the castle over the hill."

The castle cook was pleased to have help. She took pity on Prue and gave her some food.

Prue was going home when she passed the ballroom. There was Prince Alec, giving a speech to his guests.

"It might not have been so bad to marry a prince," she thought, with a sigh.

Just then, Alec turned around and saw her. "You're the hairy prince!" cried Prue.

She tried to run
away and the food fell
from her apron. The
guests began to laugh.

"I'd like to dance with
you!" said the prince and
he reached for her hand.

Prue burst into tears. She pulled her hand from the prince and fled.

But Prince Alec caught up with her. Prue looked at him closely. It was her beggar.

Don't you recognize my violin?

He took her back to the ballroom.

"Would you marry a prince now?" asked Alec.

"I would," said Prue. "But I'm already married to one!"

No more floors to scrub. Ever!

# The lost doll

It was the day of the school fair. Daisy ran from table to table, her rag doll, Ella, bumping behind her.

The toy table was the best.
Daisy propped up Ella,
so she could see too.

*Look, Ella!*

"There you are!" said
Daisy's mother. "I've been
searching for you everywhere.
It's time to go home."

❀ 211 ❀

She took Daisy's hand and led her to the car.
But Daisy had forgotten something...

"I'd like that doll," said a tall man,
pointing to Ella.

"No!" thought Ella. "I'm Daisy's."
But there was nothing she could do.

Later that evening, the man showed Ella
to his daughter.

"Look, Sophie!" he said.

"I've bought you a new doll."

"But I've got Mia," Sophie
replied, holding up her rag doll.

Her dad's face fell.

"But thank you," Sophie went on, taking Ella.

That night, as Sophie slept, Ella lay
awake in the dark, crying silent doll tears.
"What's the matter?" asked Berry,
a large brown bear.

"I miss my owner, Daisy. She left me at the
school fair by mistake. I don't belong here."

"Don't worry," said Mia. "We'll help you find Daisy."

"Th-th-thank you," sniffed Ella. "But how?"

"I've got an idea," said Berry. "Sophie must go to the same school as Daisy. If Ella gets into Sophie's school bag..."

"...she can go to school and find
Daisy," finished Mia. "Brilliant, Berry!
Let's put the plan into action tomorrow,
when Sophie's at breakfast."
But the next morning,
there was a small problem...

SOPHIE

"I'll never reach the bag," sighed Ella. "It's too high."

"We'll help!" came a cry from the top shelf. The next moment, a line of tiny monkeys came tumbling down.

"Climb aboard, Ella," cried the nearest monkey.

Ella climbed up the monkey chain. Soon, she could almost reach the bag. Then the bedroom door started to open...

"Jump!" cried the monkeys.

Ella jumped. Just in time.

As Sophie ran to catch the school bus, she never guessed who she was taking with her.

SOPHIE

At school, Sophie dumped
her bag in the classroom
and rushed off to assembly.

Ella peered out and gasped. The room
was huge. "How will I ever find Daisy?"
she wondered.

And then, at the other
end of the classroom,
she spotted Daisy's bag.

When Daisy got home, she couldn't
believe her eyes. "Look!" she cried,
"Ella's come back to me."

Meanwhile, Sophie couldn't find her new doll anywhere.

"I don't mind," she told her dad, "I only need one doll. But look at the note I found in my bag. I don't understand it…"

Dear Mia, Berry, and the monkeys,

THANK YOU!!

Ella xx

# Rapunzel

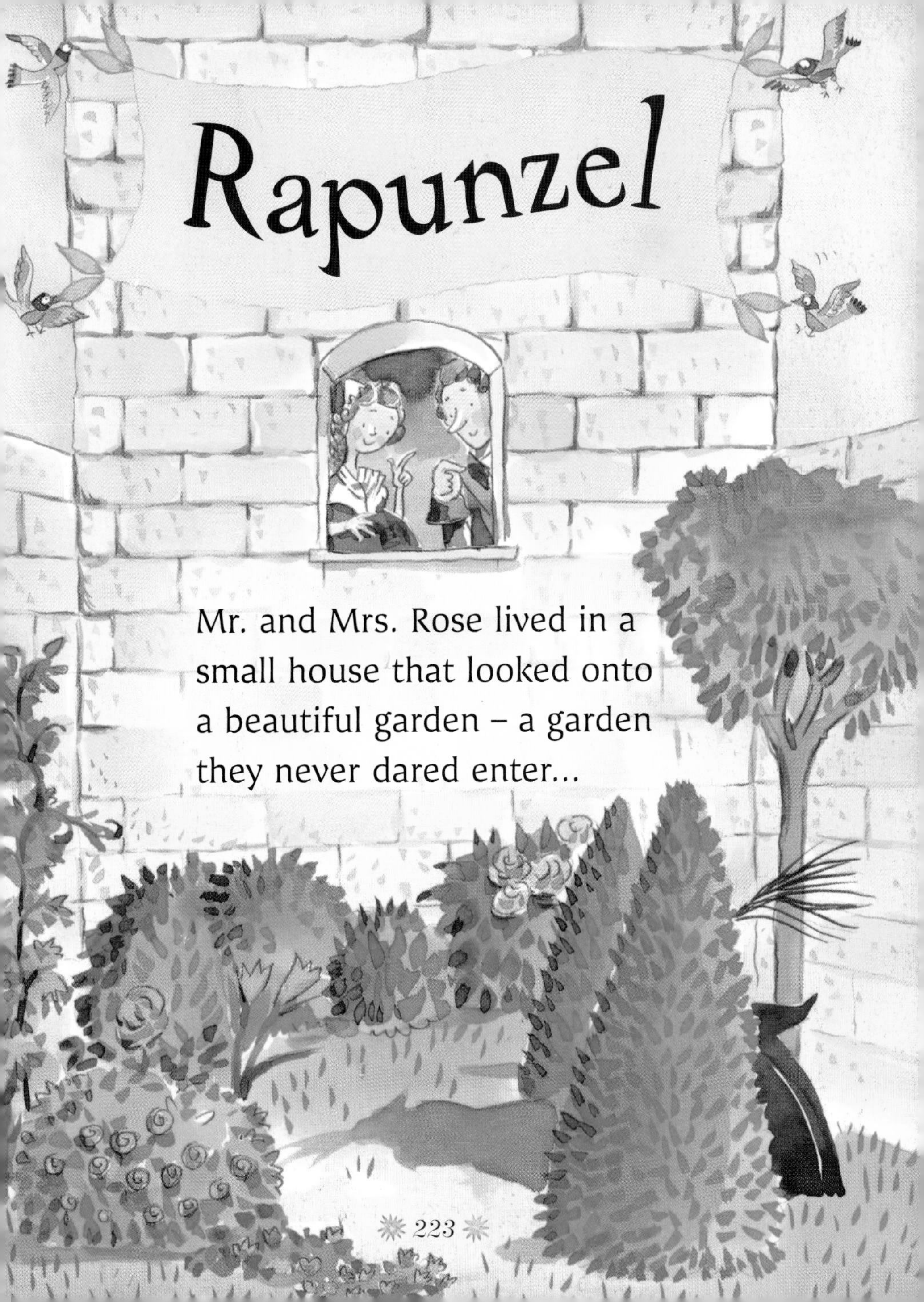

Mr. and Mrs. Rose lived in a
small house that looked onto
a beautiful garden – a garden
they never dared enter...

...because it belonged to a wicked and powerful witch.

Mrs. Rose would sit by her window and gaze at the garden for hours.

But lately, she had spent a lot of time thinking about food. "Today, I'd like chocolate pudding stuffed with spinach..." she decided.

...and minced frog.

Mr. Rose wasn't surprised. "Ever since you've been pregnant," he said, "you've wanted to eat the oddest things."

"Or perhaps," Mrs. Rose went on, "I'll have bananas, Brussels sprouts and, um, toothpaste. Oh yes, that would be lovely."

"Are you sure?" asked Mr. Rose.

"Yes," Mrs. Rose replied, "I am. Although I still think something might be missing..."

"Worms?" Mr. Rose suggested. "Or maybe you'd like some crushed ants on top?"

"Wait a moment!" Mrs. Rose cried, pointing to the witch's garden. "That's it."

"What is?"

"That vegetable. Oooh. It looks so green and juicy. I must have it!"

Mr. Rose looked. "Well you can't have it," he said. "I'm not going in that garden. The witch would eat me alive!"

"If I don't have that plant, I'll die," said Mrs. Rose and she began to cry.

After three hours of sobbing,
Mr. Rose gave in. That night,
he crept into the witch's garden.

"These vegetables all look the same in the dark," he thought. "How am I meant to know which one she wants?"

So he grabbed the nearest vegetable and raced home.

"You stupid sausage!" cried Mrs. Rose. "You've brought me a turnip."

You'll HAVE to go back again!

Next time, Mr. Rose looked carefully around the garden. "Well, this one has green leaves. It must be right," he thought. But as he pulled it out of the ground, he shuddered. A foul smell had crept up his nose.

He looked up and screamed. The witch was in front of him. Mr. Rose could smell her disgusting witchy breath.

"How dare you steal my rapunzel?" the witch cried. "I'll make you pay for this, you thieving little pimple!"

"I'll eat you alive," she hissed, a nasty glint in her eye. "I'm sure you'll be very tasty."

"P-p-please don't eat me," begged Mr. Rose.

He was shaking with fear. "I was taking it for my wife. She's about to have a b-b-baby," he stammered.

"Hmm," said the witch, thoughtfully.
"A baby?" She paused for a moment. "I'll make
a deal with you. I won't kill you and you can
have as much rapunzel as you like...

Th-th-thank you,
th-thank you,
thank you.

...but you must give me the baby
as soon as it's born."

Mr. Rose was so terrified, he agreed. He walked slowly home, shaking his head with worry. "Maybe she'll change her mind?" he thought, desperately.

But as soon as his wife gave birth to their daughter, the witch appeared.

"The child is mine," she cried. She gave a wicked grin. "And I shall call her Rapunzel, after the plant you stole. Now, give!"

Mrs. Rose wept and wept. "Don't take my baby," she pleaded.

But the witch would not give in.

She snatched the baby, and vanished.

TOO LATE! The deal is done.

Rapunzel lived with the witch for eleven years. She was treated like a slave.

GET ME TEN
SLUGS FOR MY SPELL!

The older she grew, the more beautiful Rapunzel became. She had blue eyes and long golden hair. It flowed from the top of her head...

down her back...

past her feet...

...and all along the ground.

"Rapunzel's getting too pretty," thought the witch. "I'll have to lock her away. I don't want any young men running off with her."

On the morning of Rapunzel's twelfth birthday, the witch woke her early.

"I have a lovely surprise for you," she said. "We're going to the forest for a picnic."

The forest was deep and
dark. It didn't seem a good
choice for a picnic. In the
very middle of the forest
stood a tower.

"I don't like it here,"
Rapunzel said, with
a shudder.

*Heh hehe hehe!*

"Get used to it," cackled the witch,
"because this is your new home."

The witch cast a spell, and Rapunzel found herself in a small room, at the very top of the tower.

"I can't live here," cried Rapunzel. "There's no way out – no stairs, no door..."

"You don't need to get out," said the witch, "I just need to get in. And I can climb up your hair!"

"Maybe I won't let you," said Rapunzel.

"Then you'll starve," said the witch, with a shrug. "Come on, let's try."

Rapunzel, Rapunzel, let down your hair!

Rapunzel heaved her hair out of the window. Her long locks tumbled down the tower and landed at the witch's feet.

The witch climbed up
Rapunzel's hair...

...and into the tower.

Four years went by. Rapunzel never
saw anyone, except the old witch.
She was very, very bored.

And no one in the world
knew where Rapunzel was.
Until one day...

...a young and handsome prince rode
through the forest. Rapunzel spotted
him from her window.

"Help!" she cried, as loudly as she could. "Please, help me!"

The prince looked up, astonished.

"Don't worry," he called, "I'll save you." Spurring on his horse, he galloped to the tower. "Prince Hans to the rescue!" he called.

He rode around the tower three times.
"Um, I can't find the door," he said.

"There is no door," Rapunzel
told him. "This is a magic tower.
I'm being kept here by a wicked
witch. You must climb up my hair."

"Well I've never done that before," said Prince Hans. "This is harder than it looks, you know," he added, as he began to climb. "What's your name?" he asked.

"Rapunzel," she replied.

Prince Hans almost fell off her hair, laughing.

"Just what's so funny?" Rapunzel asked haughtily.

"You've got the same name as a vegetable!" said Prince Hans, still chuckling.

"Oh," said Rapunzel, who thought her name was rather pretty. "Perhaps I'm too *funny* to rescue?"

"Not at all," said Prince Hans, as he reached the top of the tower. "But how am I going to save you?"

"You're the prince," said Rapunzel. "You think of something."

Prince Hans looked around the room thoughtfully and spotted a pair of scissors.

Gosh, I'm brilliant!

"I know!" he cried, "I'll cut off your hair, make a rope and then we can both climb down it."

"You are *not* cutting off my hair,"
said Rapunzel. "Have you any idea
how long it took to grow?"

"Fine," replied Prince Hans,
"but you'll have to come up with
a better idea, or your hair gets it."

※ 253 ※

Rapunzel thought quickly. "Visit me every night and bring a ball of silk with you. I'll weave a ladder from it."

"But that'll take ages," said Prince Hans.
Rapunzel frowned at him.
"...which isn't a problem," he added quickly.

After that, the prince came every evening. He told Rapunzel about his kingdom. "I live in a beautiful castle," he said. "There are courtyards full of fountains and flowers..."

...and turrets that touch the sky.

As the weeks passed,
Rapunzel's ladder grew longer
and longer. "Only one more
week and I'll be free..." she
thought to herself one morning.

"Rapunzel," the witch called from outside, "Rapunzel, let down your hair. I have some food for you."

As the witch climbed up, she pulled and tugged painfully on Rapunzel's hair.

"Ow!" cried Rapunzel.
"Why do you always
tug so much? Prince
Hans never hurts me when
he climbs."

WHAT?!

"Prince Hans?" shouted the witch.
"Who is Prince Hans? You *wicked* girl!
I thought I'd shut you away from the
world, but you've tricked me."

The witch leaped into the tower
and quickly grabbed a pair of scissors.
She hacked away at Rapunzel's hair
until it lay in a heap on the floor.

"I haven't finished," cried the witch.
With a powerful spell, she cast
Rapunzel into the desert.

Then the witch
waited for the
prince, a sly
smile on her
wrinkled face.

*Rapunzel, Rapunzel! Let down your hair!*

That night, Prince Hans called
out to Rapunzel as usual. Her hair
came shimmering down.

But when the prince reached the top of the tower, he gasped in shock. An ugly old crone stood in her place.

"Where's Rapunzel?" he demanded.

"Rapunzel's gone," said the witch, with a sinister laugh. "You'll never see her again."

Then the witch leaned out of the tower
and kissed Prince Hans with her slimy lips.
"Yuck!" cried the prince.

It was a magic kiss. Suddenly, the prince's
hands were covered in slime. He lost his grip
and fell to the ground like a stone.

Prince Hans landed smack in a thorn bush. It saved his life, but the sharp thorns blinded him.

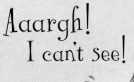

Aaargh!
I can't see!

Despite his pain, Prince Hans stood up.
"I may be blind," he shouted to the witch,
"but I'll find Rapunzel."
"Never!" she cackled.

Prince Hans wandered for months
seeking Rapunzel. At last, he met
a camel seller who told him
about a girl with golden hair
and blue eyes, living alone
in the middle of the desert.

Prince Hans hired a driver and
the fastest horses he could find.
"Take me to the desert," he said.

Rapunzel watched the carriage arrive in amazement. As Prince Hans stumbled out, she ran to him, put her arms around his neck and wept.

Two of her tears fell into Prince Hans' eyes, and he gasped. "I can see!" he cried.

"Rapunzel," he said, "I never thought I'd say this to a girl named after a vegetable, but will you marry me?"

"Oh yes!" said Rapunzel.

Prince Hans took Rapunzel to his castle. The entire kingdom was invited to their wedding, including Mr. and Mrs. Rose.

My daughter!

Princess Rapunzel and Prince Hans lived
happily together for the rest of their lives
and, in time, had three beautiful children –
Pumpkin, Lettuce and Sprout.

# THE PRINCESS AND THE PIG BOY

Once, a poor prince named Sam lived in a tiny castle. All he owned was a beautiful rose tree and a lovely nightingale.

Sam fell in love with a rich princess named Sara. So, he sent her his beautiful tree and the lovely nightingale.

But Sara was not pleased. "A silly tree and a noisy bird?" she said. "Send them back!"

Sam didn't give up. He went to Sara's palace and got a job taking care of the palace pigs.

"They don't smell as sweet as my rose tree," he thought.

But Sam missed his home. He especially missed the lovely songs of his nightingale.

So, he made a rattle which played magical tunes.

It's put the pigs to sleep!

Sara was out with her maids when she heard the rattle.

"I want it!" she said.

"It costs one hundred kisses," said Sam.

"Never!" said Sara. But she did want the rattle. "I'll give you ten kisses," she said.

"The price is one hundred," said Sam. Sara had to give in.

Yu..u..ukk!

The king was on his
balcony, when he heard
giggling. It was coming
from the pig sty.

*What's going on down there?*

The king hurried down. He crept up behind
Sara's maids and looked over their shoulders.
"Hmm, someone's kissing the pig boy,"
he said. Then he realized. "It's Sara!"

The king was very angry. "Princesses don't kiss pig boys!" he shouted. "Both of you must leave at once."

GO AND NEVER COME BACK!

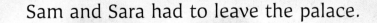

Sam and Sara had to leave the palace.

"I don't even like pigs," said Sara.
"I wish I'd married that poor prince."
Sam quickly changed his clothes
behind a tree. "You can!" he cried.

Sam took Sara to live in his tiny castle.
Sometimes, she even watered the rose tree.

276

# Fairy in a flap

Poppy was almost a perfect fairy. Her wand twinkled, her wings shone and her spells never went wrong.

But Poppy had a problem...

...she couldn't fly.

At school, her friends soared into the sky. Poppy couldn't get off the ground.

"Just keep trying," said the teacher. Poppy flapped her wings until they hurt, but she didn't even hover.

Her mother took her to the fairy doctor.
"Hmm..." he said. "Stretch out like a butterfly."
Poppy's wings fluttered open.

"She seems fine," he said, "but try
this potion." He mixed a little honey
with some fluffy clouds.

The potion was delicious, but it didn't help Poppy fly.

"How do you do it?" she asked her best friend, Daisy.

Daisy shrugged. "It just happens," she said.

"You're so lucky," said Poppy, sadly.

"Well, you're better at spells than me," said Daisy.

While her friends did aerobatics,
Poppy was stuck in the baby class.
As she flapped her wings, a tear
rolled down her cheek.

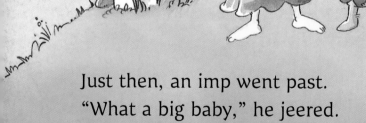

Just then, an imp went past.
"What a big baby," he jeered.

Poppy ran from the class sobbing.
She didn't stop until she reached the forest.
Still crying, she hid in a hollow tree.

"Whooo's that?" hooted an owl grumpily.
"Why the fuss?"

Hiccuping, Poppy told him.

"Imps are so rude," tutted the owl.

"As for learning to fly, I can teach you.
I've taught hundreds of fledglings."

"Jump off a low branch," he ordered, "and flap your wings."

Concentrating hard, Poppy jumped, flapped... and dropped straight to the ground.

"Oooh dear," the owl hooted. "You're thinking about it too much. Never mind. We'll try again tomorrow."

Back at home, Poppy was making a bandage
from blackberry leaves when Daisy burst in.
"I've found a spell to make you fly!"
she squealed excitedly.

Before Poppy could stop her, Daisy had waved her wand and gabbled a spell.

Leave the ground and touch the sky...
Voll-ah-ray Poppy...
...you will fly!

"I feel the same," Poppy said, doubtfully.
"Try it!" urged Daisy, pushing her through the door. "I won't watch."

Poppy went outside,
took a deep breath and
opened her wings.
Suddenly, she heard a
cry. One of the baby
fairies was stuck high
up in a sunflower.

"Hold on!" she called
and flew up to the
frightened baby.

As she fluttered back down, Daisy raced out.
"Poppy, wait. I got the spell wrong..."
She stopped. "Poppy?"

"Yes," said Poppy, with
a big grin. "I can fly!"

# The Nutcracker

A nutcracker is a wooden or metal tool for cracking nutshells. When this story was written, nuts were a special Christmas treat. Some nutcrackers were even shaped like dolls and given as presents.

This is the tale of a rather
unusual nutcracker doll...

A soft, fluffy layer of snow covered
Clara's house on Christmas Eve.

Inside, a party was in full swing,
but one very special guest hadn't arrived.
Clara watched for him at the window.

Suddenly, there was a loud
knock on the door.
"He's here!" she cried, dancing
over and flinging open the door.

It was Clara's godfather. She gave
him a big hug.

"What a warm welcome on such
a chilly night!" he said, with a chuckle.

Clara loved her godfather's visits.
Something magical always happened
when he was around.

"I have a very special present for you this year," he told Clara, as he placed a package under the tree.

That night, Clara couldn't sleep. She lay in bed thinking about her present. "It can't hurt if I just have a little peek," she thought.

Finally, Clara tiptoed downstairs. She soon found the present, tied up with a big red bow. On the ribbon there was a tag with a message.

Merry Christmas Clara,
I hope this protects you...
With love from your
godfather x

"I wonder what Godfather means," thought Clara.

Slowly, Clara untied the bow and
folded back a corner of the paper...
Inside, she found a wooden
nutcracker doll, dressed like a soldier.

Just then, the clock struck midnight.
Clara gave an enormous yawn. In a few
minutes, she was fast asleep under the tree.

Clara woke up with a start, feeling very
confused. She couldn't remember where
she was and her doll had vanished.

She looked around and
saw she was under the
Christmas tree... and it
seemed to be growing.

What's
happening?

But the tree wasn't growing – she was
shrinking. Soon, she was as small as a mouse.

Out of the corner of her eye, Clara thought she saw something leaping around. Frightened, she darted behind a present...

...and heard the tree rustle behind her. Clara spun around.

"Don't be afraid, Clara. I won't hurt you,"
said a friendly voice. Clara was astonished.

Her doll had come to life!
"I'm the Nutcracker Prince," he said,
with a bow, "and I'm here to protect you.
The kitchen mice are plotting to kidnap you."

The prince pulled out a whistle and gave a
shrill blow. At once, the lid of the
toy box flew open and a long line
of toy soldiers marched out.

Standing in rows, they saluted the prince.
"Attention!" he cried. "Clara needs our help.
Prepare yourselves for battle, men."

Wheel
out the
cannons!

Mice began to appear in the shadows. Slowly, they crept closer. Clara hid behind the prince.

"Steady, men... steady," he shouted. "Wait for the signal – and FIRE!"

Huge lumps of cheese flew from the cannons and struck down several mice. Some lumps landed in the corners and the other mice scampered after them.

"Excellent work, men!" roared the prince, as the last mouse vanished. But the fight wasn't over yet. "Bravo," said an evil voice from the shadows.

A mouse wearing a crown and an eye patch appeared.

"That's the Mouse King,"
the prince whispered to Clara.
"Is cheese the best you can do?"
jeered the king. "It'll take more than that
to beat me! Now hand over the girl."

"I'd rather die!"
said the prince.
"That can be
arranged," the
Mouse King sneered.

Soon, the prince and the Mouse King
were locked in battle. Their swords
clanged as they danced around the room.

Then disaster struck. The prince tripped on
a lump of cheese and sprawled on the floor.
Seizing his chance, the Mouse King put
his sword to the prince's neck.

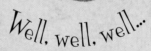

*Well, well, well...*

"I'm going to enjoy this," he said, laughing.

As the Mouse King pulled back his
sword, Clara whipped off her shoe and
threw it as hard as she could at his
head. He fell in a heap on the floor –
knocked out cold.

Clara rushed over to the prince.
"Are you alright?" she cried.
"Yes – thanks to you," he said.
"We must celebrate," he added,
as Clara helped him up.
"I know just the place."

The prince led Clara to a golden sleigh behind the Christmas tree and helped her aboard.

"Off we go, boys!" the prince called to his four reindeer.

As they gathered
speed, the sleigh
started to rise up into the
air. They rode out through an
open window and into the night.

After some time, they came to a forest covered with crisp white snow.

"We're nearly at our first stop," the prince announced. "Hold on, we're going down!"

The snow crunched under the reindeer's feet as they landed.

Just then, a beautiful lady dressed in
sparkling white appeared among the trees.

"Clara, I'd like you to meet my good friend,
the Ice Queen," said the prince.

"What a lovely surprise!" exclaimed the queen.

The queen led them to her icy palace,
which glistened in the moonlight.

Inside, icicle chandeliers hung from
every ceiling.

"You've arrived in time for the dances!"
said the queen, as they walked into a
grand ballroom.

A piano began to play and eight ballerinas dressed in silver and white twirled into the middle of the room. They twinkled like snowflakes as they spun around.

"I'll always remember this," whispered Clara to the prince, as the music came to an end.

After a game of catch with the palace poodle, it was time to leave.

"Do we really have to go?" sighed Clara.

"Yes, we really do," said the prince. "There's someone else I want you to meet and we don't have much time."

*Goodbye!*

Clara gasped when they reached their next stop. The trees were bursting with marshmallow blossoms, and lollipop flowers sprouted from the ground.

Then Clara saw that the mountains were
topped with melted chocolate and milkshake
rivers flowed down them.

"Where are we?" she asked, amazed.

"The Land of Sweets!" the prince replied.
Before them stood a huge marzipan
castle, decorated with all
kinds of treats.

Lifting Clara from the sleigh, he set her down on the palace steps and a fanfare of trumpets rang out. At the top, the doors opened and a fairy appeared, dressed from head to toe in pink.

"Clara, this is the Sugarplum Fairy," said the prince. "She rules over the Land of Sweets."

"I hope you have a sweet tooth," said the Sugarplum Fairy, with a smile.

She led them into a grand hall, where the tables were covered with chocolate cakes, cookies and candy swirls.

"Watch the wobbly chairs," whispered the prince as Clara sat down. "They're made of raspberry mousse!"

Clara ate until she thought she'd pop.

After the feast, a band struck up and dancers from around the world performed for Clara.

First came the dance of chocolate,
and a Spanish pair spun around
to snapping castanets.

Next came the exotic dance
of coffee. A beautiful Arabian
princess danced with smooth,
swirling movements in time
to soft, soothing music.

The third group of dancers had come all the way from China to entertain everyone with their tea dance.

Many more dances followed, each one showing something good to eat or drink.

But the final dance was very different.
A group of ballerinas, all dressed as flowers,
performed a slow waltz for Clara.

Their arms unfolded gracefully like
the petals of a flower, as they weaved
in and out of each other.

"And now I'm afraid it's time for us to go home," said the prince sadly. With a sigh, Clara climbed into the sleigh and waved goodbye to the Sugarplum Fairy.

"Thank you for an amazing evening, Nutcracker Prince," said Clara, with a yawn. She was so tired that she fell asleep on his shoulder.

When Clara woke up, she was back under the Christmas tree and the prince was gone.

Only her doll lay beside her.

"Oh, it was only a dream," she cried. "But it seemed so real."

Just then, Clara spotted the tag that her godfather had attached to her present.

"I hope this protects you," it said.

"I wonder if that means he knew the Nutcracker Prince would rescue me," thought Clara. "Maybe it wasn't just a dream..."

Merry Christmas Clara. I hope this protects you... With love from your godfather x

# The ghostly galleon

Harmony lived with her mother at
the very bottom of the ocean.

They were so poor they could only afford a tiny cave. This was cramped, dark and very cold. It froze their fins and took the shine off their scales.

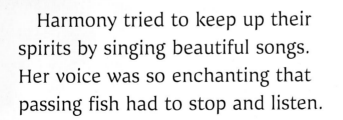

Harmony tried to keep up their spirits by singing beautiful songs. Her voice was so enchanting that passing fish had to stop and listen.

One day, Harmony's mother woke up
shivering all over. She was covered in blue
spots and her tongue had turned purple.
Harmony rushed to find Dr. Finley.

Say ahh.

Ahh....ah....ahh....ahh...aaahhh...

"Your mother is very sick," he whispered to Harmony, "The only cure is polkadot seaweed, taken twice a day for one week."

"Where can I find that?"asked Harmony.

"That's the problem," replied Dr. Finley. "It only grows in the Pirates' Graveyard."

"Oh no," gasped Harmony. "Not that spooky place full of sunken pirate ships?"

"I'm afraid so," replied the doctor.

"They say it's haunted by the ghost of Gingerbeard," said Harmony with a shiver. "He was the fiercest pirate to sail the Seven Seas."

The thought of visiting the graveyard filled
Harmony with fear, but she had no choice.
Minutes later, she was swimming
nervously between the creepy wrecks.

Harmony searched countless ships without luck. She had almost given up hope, when she saw something spotty sticking out of a rusty old cannon.

Suddenly, a
terrifying figure
appeared from
nowhere.

*Yahahahaha!*

Harmony yelped
in fright. It was
Gingerbeard's ghost.

"Come to steal my treasure, eh?"
snarled the pirate.

"No," cried Harmony. "I just need the
polkadot weed to cure my mother."

"I don't believe you," cackled Gingerbeard.
He grabbed Harmony roughly and locked
her in a cabin.

"No one gets their hands on my gold," screamed the ghost. With that, he shimmered off to patrol the top deck.

Harmony felt terrible. She tried to cheer herself up by singing, but all her songs came out sounding sad.

Harmony's lovely voice floated around Gingerbeard's ship. No matter where he went, the pirate could hear her.

However hard he tried, Gingerbeard couldn't drag himself away from the mermaid's tragic tunes.

As each day passed, he began to feel as
sorry for Harmony as a tough old pirate can.

After a week of the singing, Gingerbeard
had had enough.

"I can't take any more!" he sobbed. "Please
just go home and take this chest with you."

Harmony swam home as fast as
she could and opened the chest.
Polkadot weed floated out,
along with handfuls of coins.

Harmony's mother was cured and,
thanks to Gingerbeard's gold, they
moved into a warm and cosy new cave.

# Hans Christian Andersen

Hans Christian Andersen was born in a little town in Denmark called Odense, in 1805. His father was a shoemaker and his mother was a washerwoman, and they were very poor.

In fact, his childhood sounds very much like the beginning of a fairy tale, and just as in a fairy tale, Hans left home to seek his fortune when he was still a young boy. At first, he longed to become a famous actor, dancer or singer, but then he discovered his true purpose in life: writing.

Hans was inspired by the stories he heard in Odense as a child, where the old women still told traditional tales and half-believed them, too. He wrote fairy tales based on these stories and became famous all over the world. He died in 1875.

## Jacob and Wilhelm Grimm

Jacob and Wilhelm Grimm were brothers who lived in Germany in the early 1800s. They journeyed from village to village in the German countryside, collecting fairy tales. The Grimms published hundreds of these stories during their lifetime, gathering them into large volumes of tales. Wilhelm died in 1858 and his elder brother Jakob died in 1863. Their stories have been told time and again all over the world.

## The Nutcracker

This story was first written in 1816 by a German author named E.T.A. Hoffmann. His version of the story, called *The Nutcracker and the King of Mice*, was a dark and bitter tale. Alexander Dumas adapted the story for children, making it far less grim. But it was the ballet by Pyotr Illych Tchaikovsky that really made the story famous. *The Nutcracker* was first performed in 1892, and it is still popular today, especially around Christmas time.

Digital manipulation by Nick Wakeford,
Helen Wood and Mike Wheatley